Lucas Makes a
COMEBACK

by Igor Plohl * illustrated by Urška Stropnik Šonc

HOLIDAY HOUSE • NEW YORK

Library of Congress Cataloging-in-Publication Data

Names: Plohl, Igor, author. | Šonc, Urška Stropnik, illustrator.
Waller, Kristina Alice, translator.
Title: Lucas makes a comeback / by Igor Plohl ; illustrated by Urška
Stropnik Šonc ; English translation by Kristina Alice Waller.
Other titles: Lev rogi najde srečo. English
Description: First edition. | New York : Holiday House, [2021] | Originally
published in Slovenian in Maribor, Slovenia, by Založba Pivec in 2014
under title: Lev rogi najde srečo. | Audience: Ages 4-8. | Audience:
Grades K-1. | Summary: Lucas the lion learns how to live life with a
physical disability with help from his friends and family.
Identifiers: LCCN 2020016978 | ISBN 9780823447664 (hardcover)
Subjects: CYAC: People with disabilities—Fiction. | Wheelchairs—Fiction.
| Lion—Fiction. | Animals—Fiction.
Classification: LCC PZ7.1.P624 Luf 2021 | DDC [E]—dc23
LC record available at https://lccn.loc.gov/2020016978

ISBN: 978-0-8234-4766-4 (hardcover)

Lucas Lion loved driving, cycling, and skiing. But most of all, Lucas loved teaching the girls and boys at the Pleasantville Country Day School.

Lucas lived by himself in a little white house.

"I am king of my castle!" Lucas said.

One day, Lucas was climbing a ladder to fix his roof when he fell down hard. Lucas was in a lot of pain. And he was very scared. Lucas seriously hurt his spine, the bones in the middle of his back. Doctors fixed the injuries as best as they could. And they gave him exercises to do every day that would make him stronger. But the doctors told Lucas he would never walk again.

Did that mean Lucas would never drive or cycle or ski? Did that mean Lucas would never go back to teaching the girls and boys at the Pleasantville Country Day School?

Did that mean Lucas would never be happy again?

Then Lucas got a wheelchair to help him get around. Lucas moved back to his parents' home. His mother tidied his room, cooked his meals, and combed his mane so it was clean and shiny. His father washed and ironed Lucas's clothes.

Lucas was sad that he could no longer take care of himself.

But soon friends came to call. They comforted him,
encouraged him, and helped him any way they could.
Lucas was so glad to see them he sometimes forgot
about his troubles.

One day, Lucas's principal called him.
"Are you ready to come back to work? The children miss you!"
But how would Lucas get to work?

Lucas's friends had an idea. They all got together to raise money for a special car that Lucas could drive without using his legs.

Lucas was a teacher again! The children were happy when Lucas came back. Lucas was happiest of all!

Lucas had to learn new ways to do things. He had to learn how to get out of bed and into his wheelchair. He had to learn how to get dressed sitting down. He had to learn how to cook, clean, and iron—all from his wheelchair.

Lucas practiced and practiced until he could do it all. It was time for Lucas to move out of his parents' house and live on his own again.

But finding a home was more difficult than Lucas expected. The apartments he looked at had many steps and no ramps for Lucas's wheelchair.

And Lucas's mother worried. "Who will pick you up if you fall? If you get sick, who will take you to the doctor? Get you medicine? Make you tea?"

And then one day, Lucas got lucky. He found the perfect apartment. The building had a ramp and an elevator too.

The bathroom was large enough for his wheelchair, the sink was just the right height, and the shower could fit the special chair Lucas needed.

Everything in the kitchen was just the right height for a lion in a wheelchair.

"I am king of my castle again!" Lucas said.

Ellie Zebra went to Lucas's apartment once a week to help him clean. And Lucas met many new friends who were happy to help if he got sick or if he couldn't reach something or if the elevator wasn't working.

Soon Lucas started playing sports again—cycling, skiing, table tennis, badminton, basketball, and even scuba diving. Lucas danced again too.

Lucas learned to take good care of his body—to exercise every day and eat well.

Now Lucas's mother doesn't have to worry anymore!

In the bathroom

Getting into his car

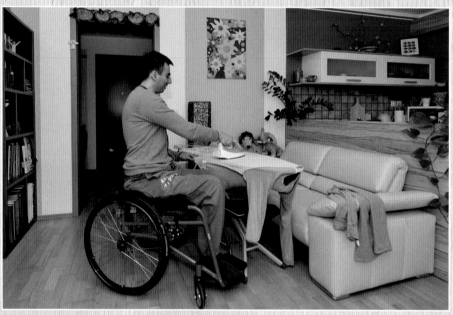
Ironing

Igor Plohl (pronounced EE-gor PLAHL) was born and raised in Slovenia, where he teaches at a primary school and lectures extensively on physical disability and spinal cord injury. After falling from a ladder at the age of twenty-nine, he injured his spinal cord and became paraplegic.